Intricate
EGGS

45 EASTER DESIGNS TO COLOR

BY CHUCK ABRAHAM

RUNNING PRESS
KIDS
PHILADELPHIA·LONDON

9   8   7   6
Digit on the right indicates the number of this printing

ISBN 978-0-7624-3178-6

Interior Illustrations by Chuck Abraham
Cover design by Ryan Hayes
Typography: Affair and Futura

This book may be ordered by mail from the publisher.
Please include $2.50 for postage and handling.
But try your bookstore first!

This edition published by Running Press Kids,
an imprint of
Running Press Book Publishers
2300 Chestnut Street
Philadelphia, PA 19103-4371

Visit us on the web!
www.runningpress.com

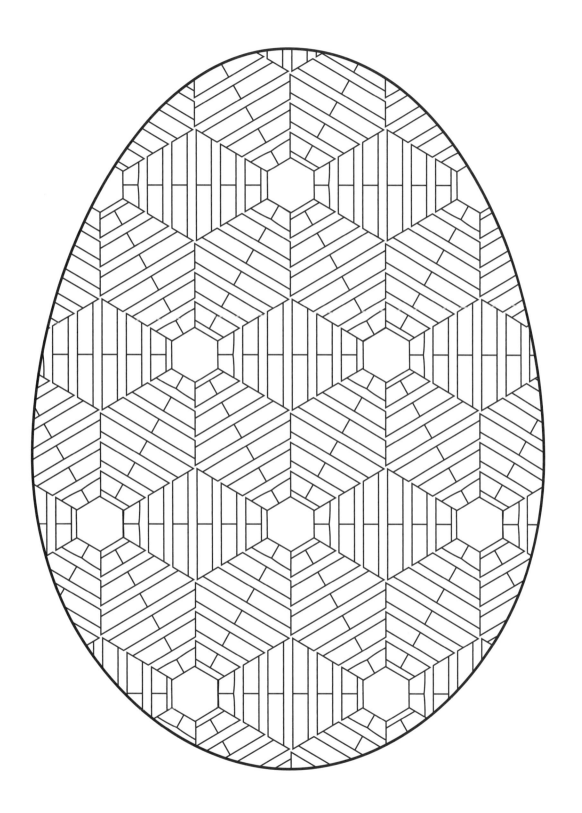

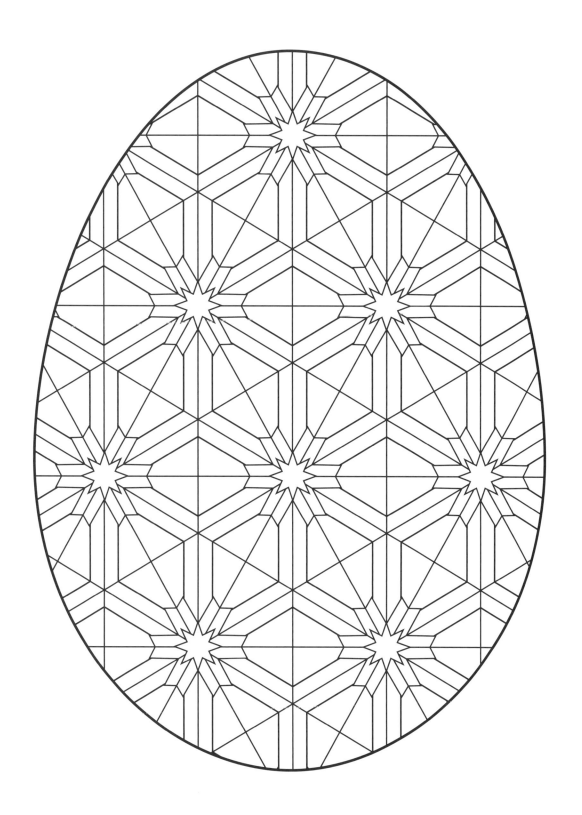

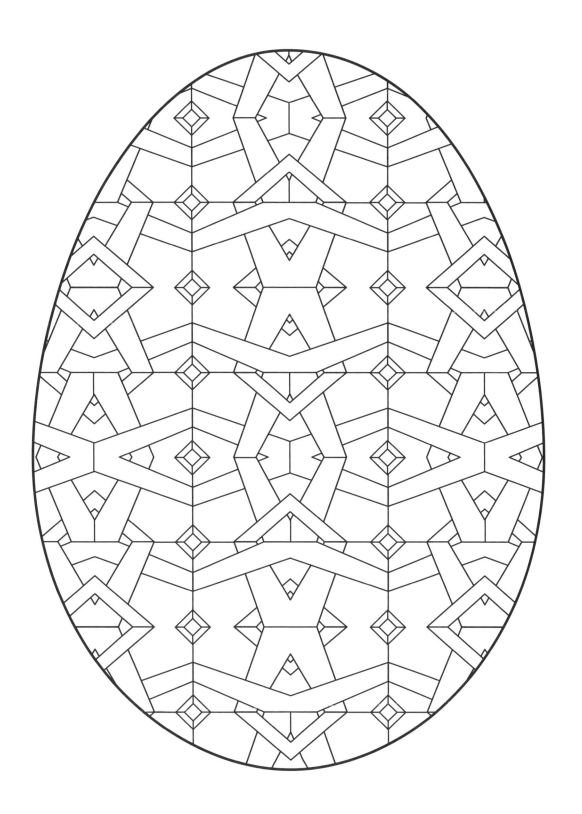

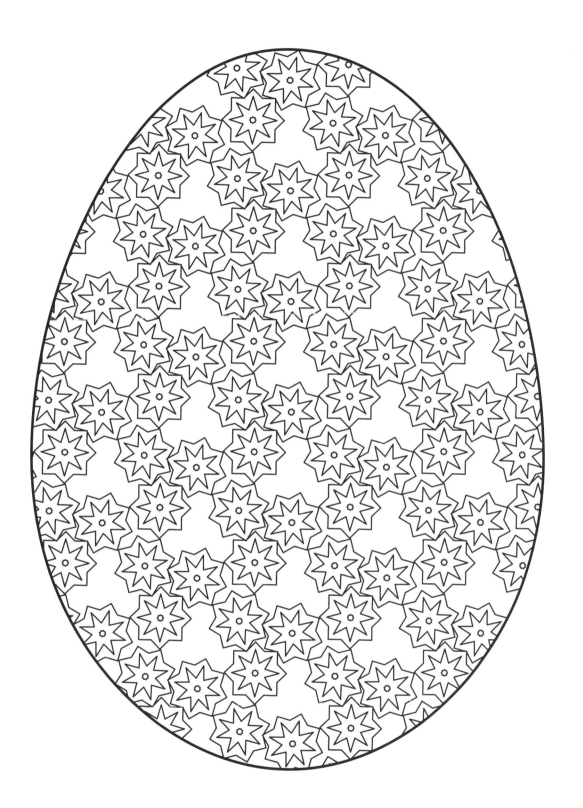

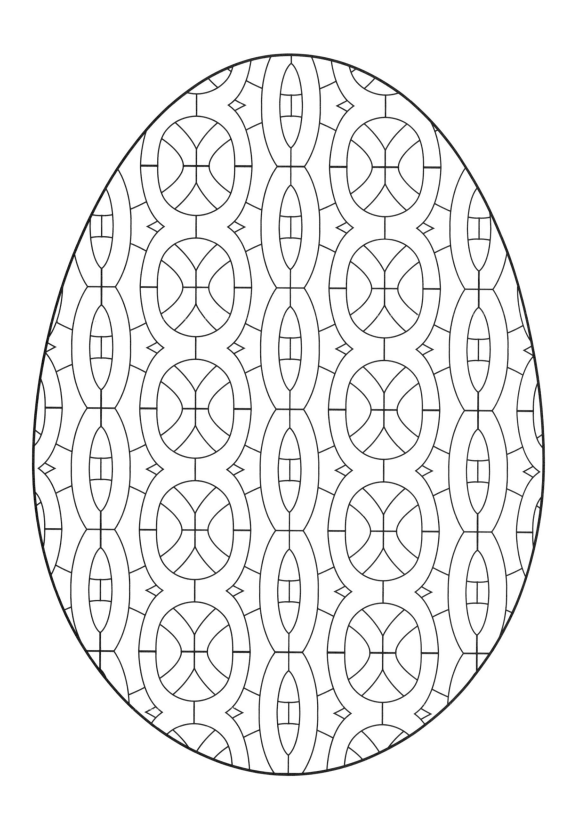

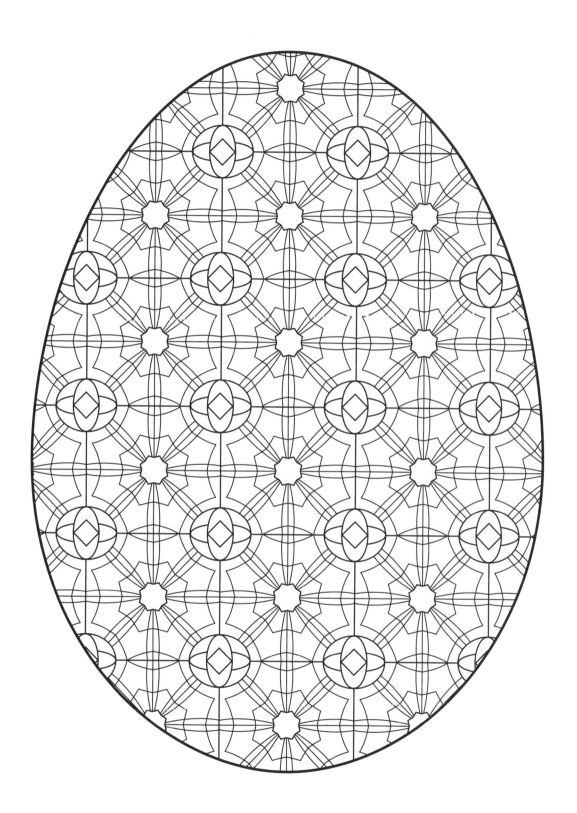

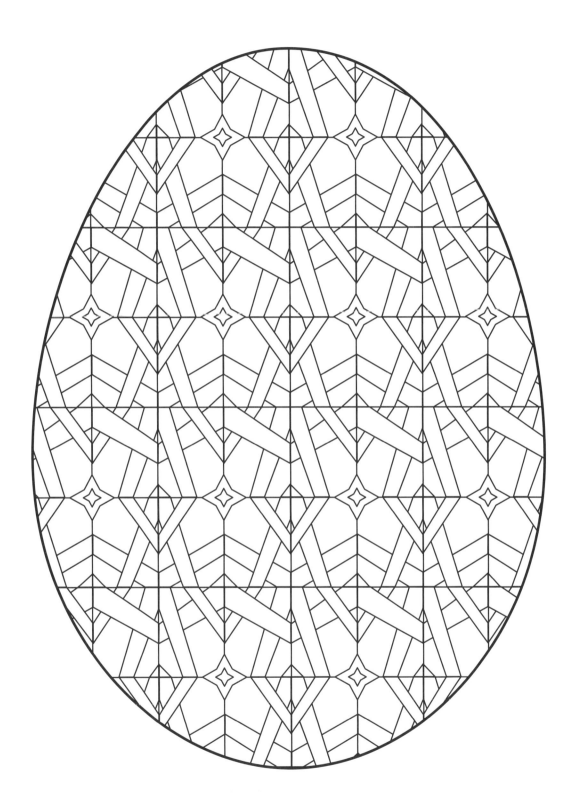

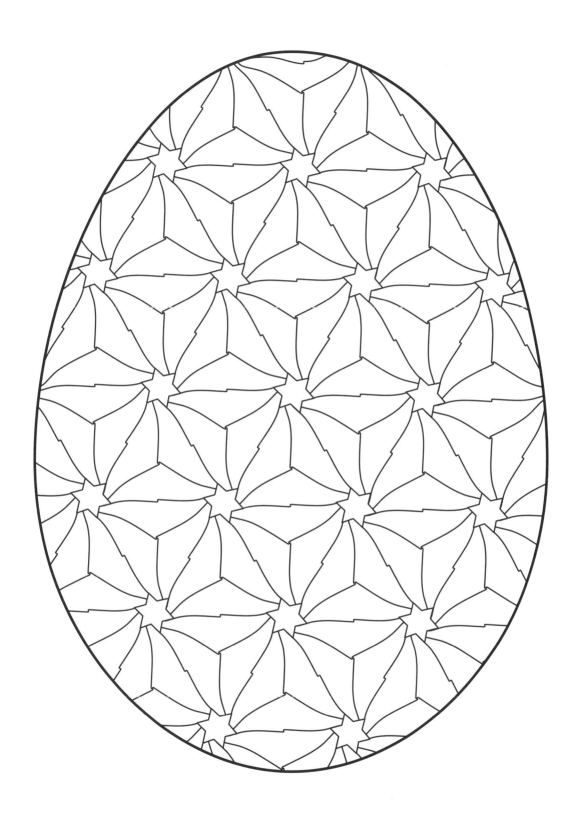

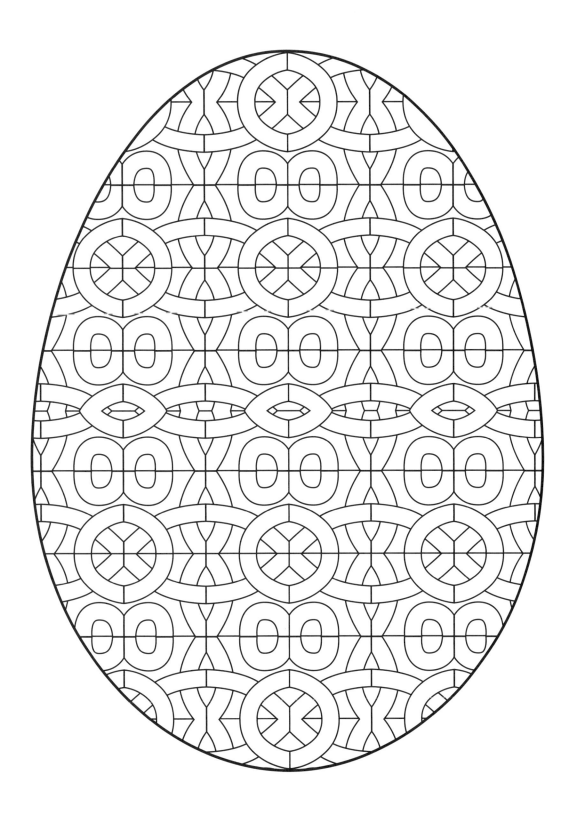

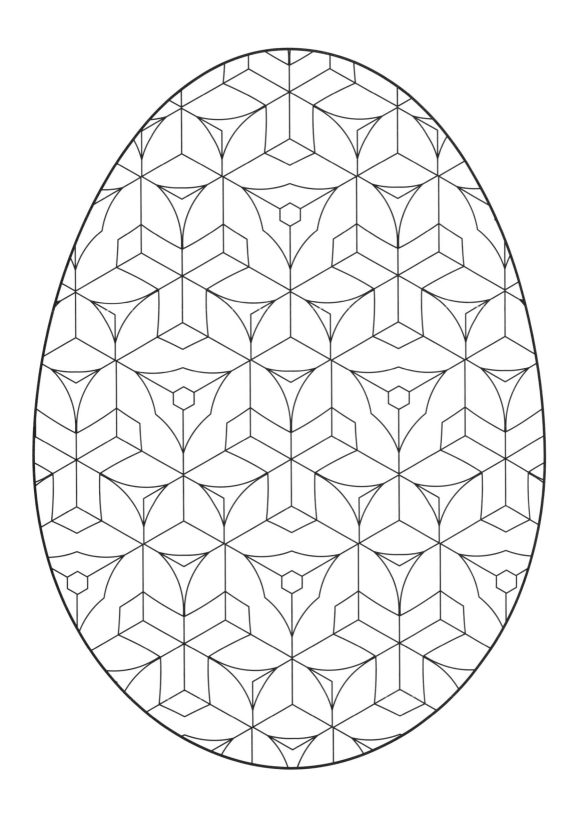

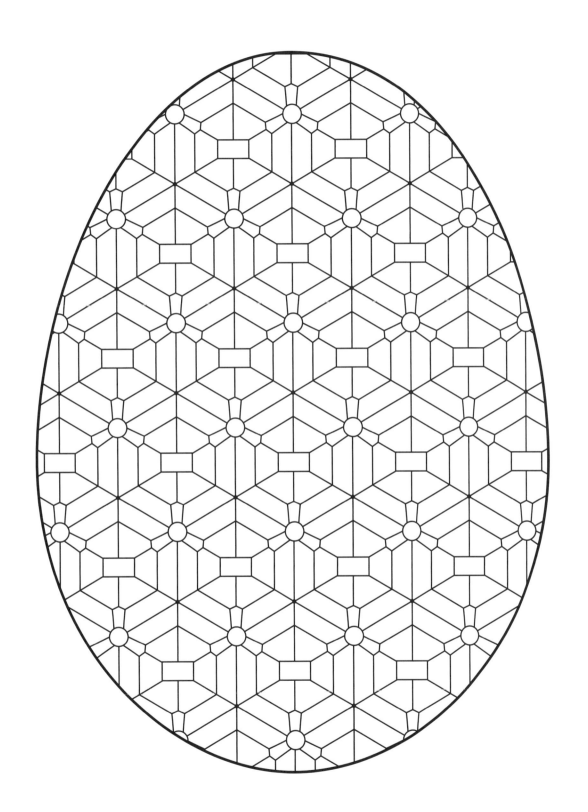

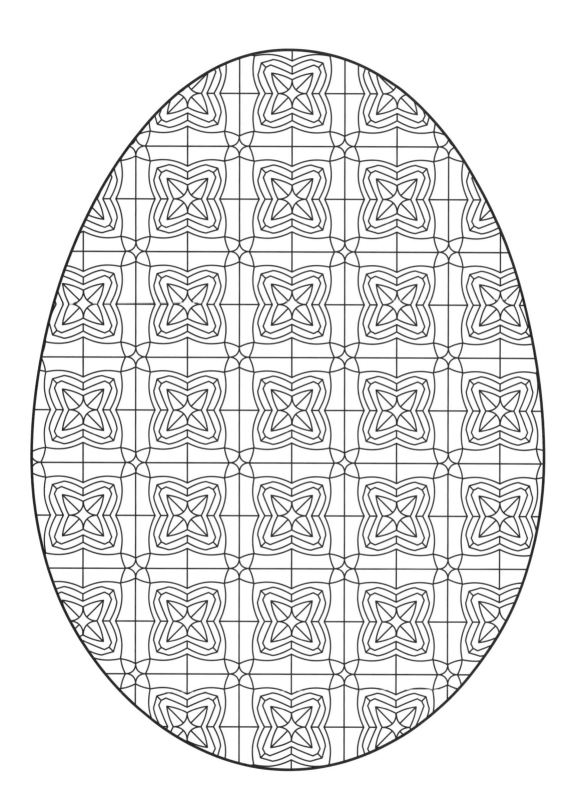

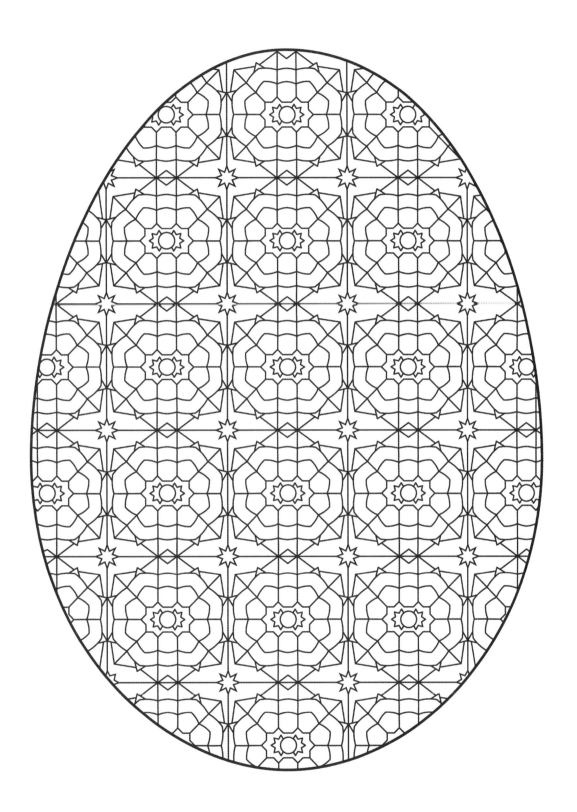